MIGHTY MORPHIN POWER RANGERS™

TIGERZORD POWER!

By Cathy East Dubowski

A PARACHUTE PRESS BOOK

A PARACHUTE PRESS BOOK
Parachute Press, Inc.
156 Fifth Avenue
New York, NY 10010

Creative Consultant: Cheryl Saban.

With special thanks to Cheryl Saban, Ban Pryor, and Sherry Stack.

Printed in the U.S.A.
January 1995
ISBN: 0-938753-89-4
A B C D E F G H I J

PROLOGUE

The battle between Good and Evil rages on!

And for the Power Rangers, the fight is tougher than ever. That's because Lord Zedd, Emperor of all Evil, is back! He banished Rita Repulsa, the Queen of Evil, from her fortress. Now he's in charge!

With his fiery moods, Zedd

frightens all who dare to come near him. And he's on a mission: to destroy the Power Rangers once and for all!

But Zordon, the good wizard who gave the Rangers their super-strength, has made them even more powerful. Jason, Kimberly, Trini, Zack, and Billy each have a new, incredible Zord charged with the power of thunder!

Tommy doesn't have a new Zord—and he might never! His powers are weakening and are in danger of fading out forever!

But the Power Rangers—including Tommy—will stop at nothing to protect the Earth. So evil forces beware! It's morphin time!

CHAPTER 1

"Hey! Where's our food?" A loudmouthed kid named Bulk pounded the counter at the Angel Grove Juice Bar. Bulk was Angel Grove's biggest troublemaker.

"Yeah," his pal Skull whined. "We don't have all day!"

Trini and her friend Billy sat at the counter sipping fruit shakes.

"Is that your excuse for being rude?" she asked quietly.

"For your information," Bulk said, "we're on a top secret mission. We're searching for the Power Rangers!"

The waiter shook his head. "Hey, guys, your sandwiches are right here." Skull grabbed the bag and sniffed inside. Bulk poked around in his. Satisfied, they stomped out of the juice bar.

"I don't think Bulk and Skull could find the Power Rangers if they were right under their noses!" Billy's blue eyes twinkled behind his glasses.

Trini giggled. She and Billy and their four best friends—Jason,

Kimberly, Zack, and Tommy—seemed liked normal teenagers. But they shared an *outrageous* secret. Whenever danger threatened the Earth, they changed—into the Mighty Morphin Power Rangers!

Just then Kimberly rushed in, waving an envelope in the air. "Guess what!" she squealed. "I got a letter from Tommy. He's coming home at the end of the week!"

Tommy had been visiting his aunt. And he'd been away for a whole month. Everyone missed him. Once Tommy had been an evil Green Ranger. Then he joined the Power Rangers to work for the forces of Good.

"Excellent!" Billy said.

"This calls for a surprise party," Trini added.

Kimberly clasped her best friend's hand. "Great idea, Trini! Come on. Let's go to the park and tell the rest of the guys!"

Angel Grove Park was rocking! Kids were jogging, rollerblading, biking—or just hanging out. Kimberly, Billy, and Trini found Zack and Jason playing football with some friends from school.

"Hey, guys," Kimberly called. "Tommy's coming home at the end of this week!"

"We're throwing a surprise party for him," Billy added.

"That's great!" dark-haired Jason said.

"Jammin'!" Zack added. "I'm in the mood for a party. It's been way too quiet around here."

Happy and excited, the friends began to make party plans.

This is great! Kimberly thought. *It's a beautiful day. Everyone's having a good time. And Tommy's coming home!* Kimberly was proud of the work she and the other Power Rangers did. But sometimes it was nice just to be normal teenagers for a change!

Far away at a secret Command Center, a small robot called Alpha 5 clicked and whirred. He stared into a glowing crystal ball. In this special viewing globe, Alpha could watch anything on Earth.

"All is safe and secure in Angel Grove, Zordon," Alpha reported.

The image of a pale face floated in a column of eerie green light. It was Zordon, the good wizard who had given the Power Rangers their superpowers.

"Excellent," Zordon said. "I suggest we use this quiet time to prepare for our secret mission. Prepare to transport to the hidden chamber. And...well, you know what to do."

"Aye-yi-yi-yi-yi!" Alpha cried. He clutched his hands to his shiny red chest. "This is so exciting!"

Alpha pattered over to the control panel and began jabbing colorful, blinking buttons and flipping switches. Lights flashed.

Zordon's face slowly changed into a ball of crackling energy. It burned brightly...then vanished.

Humming happily, Alpha turned to a keypad of numbers and punched in a code. A secret door sprang open, revealing a blaze of white light. Alpha hurried into the bright glow...and disappeared.

Then all the lights faded, and the computers blinked off. The Command Center was completely shut down!

CHAPTER 2

With a puzzled tilt of his head, Lord Zedd, Emperor of all Evil, rose slowly from his throne. His servants—Goldar, Baboo, and Squatt—trembled nearby.

Even in a quiet mood, Lord Zedd was terrifying. His huge body looked like raw red muscle bound by silver armor. Thin, clear tubes of gurgling liquid snaked around his arms and legs. No one had ever seen his face, because he hid it behind a silver mask.

Zedd's Chamber of Command was located in his castle on the moon. The chamber always changed colors to match his moods. Today it was an icy blue. Lord Zedd was at peace.

"I am detecting something quite unusual," Lord Zedd remarked. The emperor strode to his balcony. He searched Earth with the red laser beams that shot out from his eyes.

"Ah-ha!" he smirked. "Zordon and that scrap heap Alpha have left the Command Center completely unguarded! Now the Power Rangers will be powerless against us!"

Lord Zedd's evil gaze scanned Earth again until he spotted the teenagers in Angel Grove Park. He heard them planning their surprise party for Tommy.

"The time has come for us to have a little surprise party of our own for the Green Ranger," Lord Zedd sneered. "Once and for all, we will turn him over to the Dark Side!"

Zedd lifted his head high and gazed out into the universe. "But first I must create a new monster," he bellowed. "A very special monster."

Once again a red beam shot from Lord Zedd's eyes. It traveled across space and turned into a bolt of lightning that crackled down to Angel Grove Park. To a stone statue of a giant fist.

Suddenly something strange happened.

The statue began to move—as if it were breathing! Then thick green slime oozed from its cracks.

"Perfect!" Lord Zedd cried. "My new monster! I will call it Nimrod!"

The walls of his fortress rang with his evil laughter. "Now all Nimrod needs is a little time to bake. Then we'll throw our *final* farewell party for the Green Ranger!"

CHAPTER 3

CHOMP! Bulk took a sloppy bite of his huge tuna sandwich and washed it down with a slug of orange soda. Then he wiped his mouth with the back of his hand. "See anything?" he asked Skull, who sat beside him in Angel Grove Park.

Skull peered through his binoculars at a swarm of ants trying to move some crumbs. "Nah."

Bulk and Skull had seen a flash of lightning by the statue at the end of the park, but that was quite a way off.

Skull was getting bored. "Come on, Bulky. Let's go home."

"Patience, Skull!" Bulk said. "This is where the Power Rangers were last seen."

Skull chewed on a piece of grass and sighed. "Don't you wish we had some kind of sign to show us we're on the right track?"

NEERRROOM! Something big smashed down from the sky— almost right in front of them! Bulk and Skull jumped with a shriek.

"Skull!" Bulk cried. "This is the sign we've been waiting for! Come on! Let's go check it out!"

In another part of Angel Grove Park, Jason, Trini, and their friends froze in the middle of the football game. They had heard the crash, too.

"Hey, what was *that?*" Zack exclaimed.

Jason pulled Billy aside. "Let's go check it out."

Billy nodded. "We'll be right back," he called to the others.

Then he and Jason jogged off toward the hill where they'd heard the mysterious explosion.

* * *

In the meantime Bulk and Skull had reached the crash scene. They discovered a strange container sticking up out of a smoking hole in the ground. It looked kind of like a trash can hacked from rock. Strange symbols were carved in the lid.

"This is it!" Bulk cried. "It must be a sign from outer space. I've got a strong feeling that *this* will help us find the Power Rangers!"

Skull grinned, then frowned. "Did you hear that?" He leaned closer to the strange, flying Dumpster. "It sounds like snoring."

"It must be the engine of the rocket cooling down," Bulk assured him. "Come on, Skull. Let's get this thing out of here."

Bulk and Skull heaved the weird-looking Dumpster out of the hole. Grunting and sweating, they hauled it off to Skull's house.

A minute later Billy and Jason arrived at the crash site. But all they found was the smoking hole.

Jason frowned. "What do you think, Billy?"

Billy dropped to his knees to study the hole. He touched the ground. "It's still hot," he reported. "Most peculiar. I'd say something sort of round was definitely here. And not too long ago."

"What was it?" Jason wondered aloud. "And where is it now?"

Back on the football field,
Zack threw a pass to one of the
players. He missed it, and the ball
disappeared through the trees.

"I'll get it!" Zack called.

He pushed his way through
some bushes and trees and spotted the ball. It lay near the statue
of the giant fist. Zack ran over and

scooped up the football.

"Ick!" he said in disgust. Smelly green slime dripped from the ball.

Zack stared up at the statue.

The same green slime oozed and dripped from the marble fist!

Something creepy was up. Zack ran back to the game. "Uh, hey, guys," he said to his friends, "let's call it a day. I'm bushed."

As soon as their other friends left, Kimberly asked, "What's the matter, Zack? You never get tired."

"Something's wrong." He led the girls to the statue.

"Oh, gross!" Kimberly cried, wrinkling her nose at the sight of the slime.

"We'd better contact Zordon,"

Zack said. He spoke into his communicator. "Zordon, come in."

No answer.

"Zordon? Alpha?"

Still no answer.

Zack, Kimberly, and Trini radioed Jason and Billy. "Meet us at the statue near the football field. Hurry!"

Seconds later Jason and Billy teleported to the statue.

"Hey, what *is* this stuff?" Jason exclaimed.

But before they could examine the statue, dozens of Putties suddenly surrounded them! They were Lord Zedd's warriors— brainless creatures made of dull gray clay. The Putties waved their arms wildly as they prepared to attack.

Zack leaped into a karate stance. "I guess I was wrong about it being quiet around here!"

The Power Rangers had fought Super Putties before. Every Super Putty had a Z carved on its chest. And there was only one way to defeat each deadly creature. Kick that Z!

"Prepare to destroy some real slime!" Kimberly cried.

The Power Rangers flew into action. Billy somersaulted into three Putties. Two tumbled out of the way, and his elbow connected with the third one's Z.

The Z glowed like a neon sign.

The Putty's whole body lit up. It crumbled into chunks, like a broken clay statue. Finally the Putty pieces vanished from sight.

"One down!" Billy cried out.

Kimberly sent another Putty a flying side kick. "Hiii-yaah!" she cried as her foot smashed his *Z*. Another Putty destroyed!

Then four Putties closed in on Zack. He spun around as if he were on a dance floor. "This is your last dance, Putties!" he shouted. His fist struck out as he counted to the beat: "One! Two! Three! Four!"

Four blows to four *Z*'s—four Putties crumbled.

The Power Rangers quickly

glanced around. The rest of the Putties had vanished.

"Something's definitely weird here!" Billy said.

Kimberly shuddered. "That statue gives me the creeps. And why can't we reach Alpha or Zordon?"

"Let's try again," Trini said.

Jason made the call. "Zordon! Alpha! Come in."

Nothing but empty static.

"Let's teleport to the Command Center to see what's going on," Trini suggested.

In a flash the Power Rangers were gone. So they didn't see the statue's green slime harden into a face that looked like an eerie white mask. They didn't see real eyes form, blink open, and close. They didn't see the statue coming alive!

"I don't get it," Zack gasped a few minutes later. He shook his head as he and the other Power Rangers searched Zordon's Command Center. No one was there. Everything was dark and quiet. All the computers were shut down. Even the viewing globe was dimmed. "Why would Zordon and Alpha take off and not tell us?" Zack wondered out loud.

"Billy," Trini asked, "have you found anything yet?"

Billy hurried over with a CD-ROM disk in his hand. "This disk is like a diary of everything that goes on here. With it I should be able to figure out the Command Center's activity. But the systems are all down. I'll have to take it to my lab to read it."

"Man," said Zack. "Too many weird things are going on."

"I know," Kimberly agreed. "That explosion, the slimy statue, the Putties...and now Zordon and Alpha gone!"

"Let's transport to Billy's lab and figure something out," Jason said.

The Power Rangers vanished in a streak of sparkling lights.

Many miles away Tommy dived into the brisk water of a mountain lake. Ahhh! Swimming every day was a favorite part of his visits to his aunt's house.

After a good long swim, Tommy came ashore and headed for his towel. It was right where he'd left it. He picked up the towel—and stared in wonder!

A mysterious crystal lay on the ground. *Where did that come from?* Tommy said to himself.

Then the crystal began to glow....

And a strange power locked onto Tommy's arms and legs. He groaned as he fought to break free. But he was trapped! He cried out as a bright light swallowed him up!

CHAPTER 5

Billy's hands flew over the keys of his home computer. "Interesting," he said as he read the data. "There seems to be a hidden door in the Command Center. The disk shows the controls Alpha used to open it."

BOOM! Billy's house was rocked by an explosion!

"Sounds like it came from the park," Zack said. "Let's check it out!"

Jason nodded. "It's morphin time!"

The air crackled with electricity as the five teenagers raised their Power Morphers to the sky. Just as Zordon had taught them, they called upon the spirits of the ancient dinosaurs.

"Tyrannosaurus!" "Pterodactyl!" "Mastodon!" "Saber-toothed Tiger!" "Triceratops!" In a flash the five teenagers morphed into Power Rangers.

Now they stood dressed in shining helmets and sleek jump-suits—five powerful protectors.

Jason, the Red Ranger. Kimberly, the Pink Ranger. Zack, the Black Ranger. Trini, the Yellow Ranger. And Billy, the Blue Ranger.

The Power Rangers set out to search Angel Grove Park.

"Look!" Jason cried, pointing at the slimy statue.

It had turned into a strangely beautiful monster. The creature's face took the form of a calm white mask. Its arms and legs were painted red, and they looked slender but powerful. In its hand the monster carried a staff with a colorful jeweled head.

"Be careful," Jason warned. "Without Zordon and Alpha, we have no idea what it can do."

Tommy has been away on vacation for a whole month. All the Power Rangers miss him—but he'll be home very soon!

Kimberly and Billy plan a big surprise party for Tommy's return.

"The time has come for us to have a little surprise party of our own for the Green Ranger," Lord Zedd sneers.

Meanwhile, Alpha prepares to shut down the Command Center. He and Zordon are off to work on a secret mission.

Bulk and Skull have a mission of their own—to discover the secret identities of the Power Rangers!

While Lord Zedd tells his warriors about the newest monster he plans to unleash on the Power Rangers...

...the Super Putties attack Earth!

Trini, Billy, Kimberly, Jason, and Zack morph into action!

The Power Rangers are called to the Command Center. Alpha is about to reveal his top secret project—a new Ranger!

It's a White Ranger! But who is the teen behind the white mask?

It's Tommy! He shall control the fierce Tigerzord, and his weapon shall be the Sabba Sword!

Time for Tommy, the White Ranger, to join the Power Rangers in their battle against Evil!

The creature spotted them and bowed as if to start a dance. Then it swung its staff—and blasted the Power Rangers!

All five Power Rangers tumbled to the ground.

Another blast!

"Watch out!" Jason cried. Behind them a tree exploded.

"We can't get close enough to fight it!" Kimberly cried.

"I'll make sure you *never* get close to my monster!" Lord Zedd bellowed as he watched from his castle on the moon.

A small silver bomb appeared in his raised hand. "Grow, Nimrod, grow!" he cried as he hurled the bomb down to Earth.

The bomb exploded in flames at Nimrod's feet. Then the monster grew...till it towered high in the sky.

Jason held the others back. "We need our Thunderzords!"

"Mastodon Lion Thunderzord Power!" Zack cried.

"Pterodactyl Firebird Thunderzord Power!" Kimberly cried.

"Triceratops Unicorn Thunderzord Power!" Billy shouted.

"Saber-toothed Tiger Griffin Thunderzord Power!" Trini cried.

"Tyrannosaurus Red Dragon Thunderzord Power!" Jason cried.

Roaring to life, the Zords streaked through fire and lightning to answer the Power Rangers' call.

Clang! The Zords came together to form Mega Thunderzord!

The Power Rangers jumped into the cockpit in the giant Zord's chest. "Mega Thunderzord! Power up!" they shouted.

Mega Thunderzord's eyes flashed yellow. It was ready for battle. Now it was a fair fight!

"Oh, no!" Trini cried. "Look!"

Nimrod flung its arms wide— and two more monsters appeared. They looked exactly like Nimrod! Now it was three monsters against one Mega Thunderzord!

Then Nimrod brought its hands to its lips—as if to blow a kiss.

But when it turned its palms out, lightning flashed from them.

The Mega Thunderzord stumbled. "Hang on!" Jason cried.

The two new monsters flashed their swords. Red and gold lightning crackled from the tips.

The blasts struck hard. Mega Thunderzord crashed to the ground!

The Power Rangers struggled to hang on to the controls.

Zack cried, "Our Zords! They're damaged! We need more power!"

"Billy," Jason said. "Teleport to the Command Center! See if you can find Zordon. Maybe he's back. We haven't got much time!"

CHAPTER 6

Billy's boots echoed in the dark Command Center. He shined a flashlight across the silent computer panels. At last he found the keypad of numbers he was searching for.

He pushed several buttons: 1, 2, 9, 6,*—the same code he had found on the CD-ROM disk.

It worked! A dazzling light flashed behind him. Billy whirled around. A secret door revealing a brilliant glow lay open before him.

Billy felt nervous as he hurried toward it. But he bravely stepped into the bright rays. And then…

"Aagghhh!" Billy fell down a windy tunnel of bright green light.

Moments later he landed on a black polished floor. He was surrounded by darkness. But ahead of him light shone through a square window in the floor.

Cautiously Billy crept toward the window on his hands and knees. Slowly he peeked down.

His eyes popped wide open. "Amazing!" he whispered.

In a room below he saw Alpha working over a glowing beam of light. Billy could just barely see the tip of a white boot. A gloved white hand. A white helmet.

Billy gasped!

A new Ranger!

Alpha was shaping a new Ranger out of white light!

Billy had to talk to his friends— immediately. He quickly called Jason on his communicator.

"Meet me at my lab," Billy whispered. "I've got important news!"

Within minutes the Power Rangers met at Billy's lab.

"This better be good," warned Zack. "That monster is triple the trouble, and we let it get away!"

Billy assured his friends that what he had to say was big news—news that would shock them. But how could he tell them?

"Come on, Billy," Kimberly urged. "Tell us!"

Billy took a deep breath. "Zordon and Alpha are in a hidden chamber," he said at last.

"And—?" Kimberly prompted.

Billy blurted out, "They're making a new Power Ranger!"

For a moment silence filled the room. The five teens were stunned. Then everyone started asking questions at once.

"Are you sure?" Zack asked.

"Who is it? Do you know?" Kimberly demanded.

Jason shook his head in amazement. "That's why the Command Center was shut down."

"Why can't Tommy have these new powers?" Kimberly blurted out. "He's already one of us."

"Kim's right," Zack put in. "I mean, who is this new guy?"

"I'm sure Zordon has a good reason for this," Jason said.

"Jason's right," Billy said. "Lord Zedd's monsters are far superior to Rita's. We *need* a new Ranger— no matter who it is."

The others had to admit that Billy made sense. But somehow they couldn't help but feel sad that their group was changing.

And a little worried, too.

CHAPTER 7

"We can't just sit here," Trini cried, "while the monster attacks Angel Grove!"

"But we really need the new Ranger," Billy insisted.

"Trini's right," Jason said.

"Okay, let's get that monster," Zack shouted.

Suddenly their communicators

went off. "Power Rangers!" they heard Zordon say. "Teleport to the Command Center immediately!"

"We're on our way," Jason responded.

Jason gazed at each Power Ranger—Kimberly, Zack, Trini, Billy. They'd been through a lot together. In fact, they could hardly remember what their lives had been like before they became Power Rangers...before they were a team.

But now their lives were about to change. Would they like this new Power Ranger?

"Remember," Billy pointed out, "Zordon knows what he's doing."

Kimberly wore a funny look on her face—as if she were being forced to eat her least favorite vegetable. "Well, come on, guys," she said at last. "Let's get this over with."

"At least this place is back to normal," Kimberly commented as the five teenagers arrived at the Command Center. Lights were blinking. The computers were back on-line. And once again Zordon floated in his column of eerie green light.

"This is a special occasion, Power Rangers," Zordon said. "You are about to meet the newest member of your team."

The Power Rangers tried to smile politely.

"As you know," Zordon went on, "the Green Ranger's power was completely destroyed over the last few battles."

Kimberly blinked back a tear.

"Alpha and I felt it was time to create an even more powerful Ranger," Zordon said. "One who could combat Lord Zedd's strong Evil. Alpha, please begin."

Alpha pushed several buttons on the control panel. Then the robot announced, "I now present—the White Ranger!"

A blinding white spotlight blazed down upon the Power Rangers. They gazed up, but they could barely see the human shape suspended like a puppet in the center of the light. Slowly the light lowered the new Power Ranger to the floor.

This new Ranger was dressed in a suit like theirs. But it was dazzling white and trimmed in gold.

The White Ranger was awesome! *But who was it?*

The Power Rangers stared.

The White Ranger reached up to remove the gleaming helmet.

He grinned at the startled Power Rangers. "Guess who's back?"

Kimberly took one look at the new Power Ranger—and fainted!

CHAPTER 8

It was Tommy! He was the new White Ranger!

Jason, Trini, Zack, and Billy stood speechless as the new Ranger flashed them a dazzling smile. This was better than any of them had dared to dream!

Then Tommy kneeled down at Kimberly's side.

Kimberly's eyes slowly opened. "Tommy—is it really you?"

"In the flesh," he said, laughing.

Kimberly reached up to give him a huge hug. Then Tommy helped her to her feet.

Jason spoke for them all. "We really missed you, Tommy."

"All this human emotion!" Alpha cried. "I'm going to rust."

"So, Power Rangers," Zordon spoke up at last, "I take it you're pleased with the new addition to your team?"

"This is the best!" Jason exclaimed. "We're all together again."

"But, Zordon, how?" Kimberly asked. "I mean, I thought Tommy lost his powers for good."

"The *Green* Ranger's powers are gone for good," Alpha said.

"Tommy proved himself to be worthy and true," Zordon explained. "His courage and strength enabled us to choose him to be the White Ranger. This time his powers have been created in the Light of Goodness. They can never be taken away by evil forces."

"Tommy shall control the White Tigerzord," Alpha added. "A new Zord of strength and fierceness. His power weapon shall be called the Sabba Sword."

Alpha pushed a button and Tommy's new, gleaming weapon

floated in the air before them.

"Take it, Tommy," Zordon said.

Tommy reached out and grasped the sword. He was silent for a moment. Then he smiled. "It's great to be back!"

ZZZZZzzz! Bulk and Skull hunched over the Dumpster in Skull's dad's garage. They were trying to drill a hole in it. But that didn't work. So next they tried a chain saw.

"Get me out of here!" a tiny voice suddenly cried from inside.

Skull cut the motor. "Hey, did you hear that?"

"Hear what?" asked Bulk.

Skull looked around. "Mom? Is

that you?" he called out.

Bulk and Skull shrugged and went back to sawing.

At last they gave up. "We've tried every tool your dad has," Bulk complained. "But we still can't get this thing open!"

Skull scratched his head. "Let's go to the juice bar. I've got an idea!"

Half an hour later Bulk and Skull returned with a can opener. A six-foot-tall can opener! Ernie, the juice bar owner, had once used it in a store display.

Bulk hooked the can opener onto the Dumpster. "Okay, Skull," Bulk crowed, "prepare to learn the secrets of the Power Rangers!"

CHAPTER 9

Beep! An alarm rang in the Command Center. All six Power Rangers snapped to attention.

"Nimrod and its clones are attacking," Zordon announced.

"Our Zords were damaged in the last battle we had with Nimrod!" Jason exclaimed.

Alpha stared into the viewing

globe. "Oh, no! Bulk and Skull are about to open Rita's Dumpster!"

When Lord Zedd had overthrown Rita, he had locked her in a Dumpster and flung her into orbit.

"We've got to stop them," Zack said, "before Rita reveals who we are!"

"Trini, Billy," Zordon said, "teleport to the Zords and begin repairs. The rest of you, make sure Rita does not escape!"

"Tommy," Zordon continued, "you must battle Nimrod and its clones. Go now, all of you!"

Tommy, the new White Ranger, appeared on a hillside in Angel Grove. He spotted Nimrod and its clones attacking the city.

Quickly he raised his Sabba Sword. "Tigerzord Power—*now!*"

Tigerzord answered with a roar. It clawed the ground, then bolted across the rocky Earth.

But suddenly the Tigerzord stumbled. It toppled over backward, then crashed to the ground.

"Zordon!" Tommy called. "I can't control the Tigerzord!"

Meanwhile the Pink, Black, and Red Rangers raced through Angel Grove to Skull's house. But they hit a traffic jam—of Super Putties!

One by one they tackled the Putties and hit their *Z*'s. One by one the Putties crumbled away.

Now to stop Bulk and Skull! But suddenly they received a call.

"Power Rangers," Zordon said, "Tommy's in trouble! Teleport to Trini and Billy to help repair the Zords. Deal with the Dumpster later. This is an emergency!"

The Power Rangers quickly repaired the Zords. They united them into the Mega Thunderzord and jumped into its cockpit.

Mega Thunderzord jetted through the air as Tommy managed to bring Tigerzord back on its feet. Mega Thunderzord landed on the mighty Tigerzord's back— and together they formed an incredible fighting machine!

Lord Zedd's three monsters attacked from all sides.

They fired, blast after blast, at Mega Thunderzord and Tigerzord.

Then Mega Thunderzord jumped to the ground. It watched as Tigerzord began to grow and grow. Tigerzord transformed into a super-sized figure that towered over the three monsters.

The super-sized Tigerzord raised its Sabba Sword and slashed away at Zedd's monsters. Each of the creatures fell, defeated.

"What a team!" Kimberly cheered.

But their celebration was brief. One tiny matter still remained— Rita and the Dumpster!

CHAPTER 10

Bulk threw the giant can opener to the ground. "Let's face it, Skull. We're never going to get this tuna can opened."

They slumped to the floor, their backs to the table that held the strange Dumpster. The floor was littered with tools.

"Look at this mess," Skull said.

"My dad's gonna kill me."

Behind them the lid of the Dumpster slowly opened. Two pointy cones poked out. Then a tiny Rita Repulsa stood up and stretched.

"Ahhh!" she said. "I'm *free!*"

Bulk and Skull gulped, then slowly turned around.

Bulk screamed and fainted. Then Skull, who usually did whatever Bulk did, screamed and fainted, too.

"Oh, great," Rita groaned. "A human Squatt and Baboo!"

Suddenly six beams of colored light sparkled in the room. The Power Rangers!

"Oh, no—not *you* again!" Rita

cried when she saw them.

The six Power Rangers surrounded her. Zack picked up the tiny, squealing witch and popped her back into the Dumpster.

"No-o-o!" she shrieked. "I'll get you for this!"

Tommy slammed on the lid. "We'd better get this to Zordon."

"Kim and I will stay here to make sure Bulk and Skull are all right," Trini suggested.

The four guys vanished with Rita in her mini-prison.

Before Bulk and Skull woke up, the Pink and Yellow Rangers transformed into "ordinary" Kimberly and Trini.

The girls shook the guys' shoulders, trying to wake them up.

"Two more minutes, Mommy," Bulk mumbled. "Then I'll get up."

Kimberly tried not to giggle. "Hey, are you guys okay?"

Bulk and Skull bolted upright. "There's a little witch back there behind us!" Skull whined.

"What *are* you talking about?" Kimberly said.

Bulk and Skull slowly glanced back. "She's gone!" Bulk gasped.

"Wh-where did she go?" Skull stuttered.

Kimberly and Trini stared at them as if they were crazy.

Skull blushed a deep red.

"Everything's fine," Bulk said in a strangled voice. Who'd believe a story about a tiny witch in a trash can?

At the Dumpster's crash site in the park, Billy, Tommy, Zack, and Jason watched the sunset flood the sky with color.

"Hold the Dumpster up high," Zordon instructed them.

The Power Rangers raised it toward the sky.

"Now...say good-bye!" Zordon said lightly.

"See you later, Rita!" the guys cheered together.

A field of energy surrounded the Dumpster. Then it streaked into orbit in outer space. Rita was back where she belonged.

CHAPTER 11

"**Surprise!**" Kimberly, Zack, Billy, Jason, and Trini shouted extra-loud. The teens and their friends were finally celebrating Tommy's homecoming with a party at the juice bar.

Tommy was actually blushing! "You guys are the best!"

Just then one of their friends

from school came in. His name was Richie, and he was holding a karate trophy.

"Where'd you get the trophy?" Trini asked. "Did you win it?"

"Yep," he boasted. "In a karate tournament this afternoon."

"How about showing us your winning moves?" Tommy suggested.

It took some coaxing. But at last Richie stood up and started a flying kick—just as Ernie brought out a big "Welcome Back, Tommy" cake.

"Ooops!" Richie kicked the cake—and it went flying through the air.

But Bulk and Skull came in just

in time to catch it—in their faces!

The kids all laughed.

Bulk scowled and began to wipe off the mess dripping down his cheeks. Skull tasted the icing and grinned. "Delicious!"

"Bulk and Skull really take the cake!" Zack joked.

"It's good to know some things never change," Tommy added.

The Power Rangers—all *six* of them—shared a secret smile. Together they'd been through a lot of changes. But as long as they stayed best friends, they knew they'd be fine. Especially with the new White Ranger on their team!